THIS IGLOO BOOK BELONGS TO:

....

igloobooks

Published in 2015
by Igloo Books Ltd
Cottage Farm
Sywell
NN6 0BJ
www.igloobooks.com

Cover designed by Matt Hamilton
Interiors designed by Sam Ross
Edited by Mike Heron

HUN001 1115
2 4 6 8 10 9 7 5 3 1
ISBN: 978-1-78557-063-6

Printed and manufactured in China

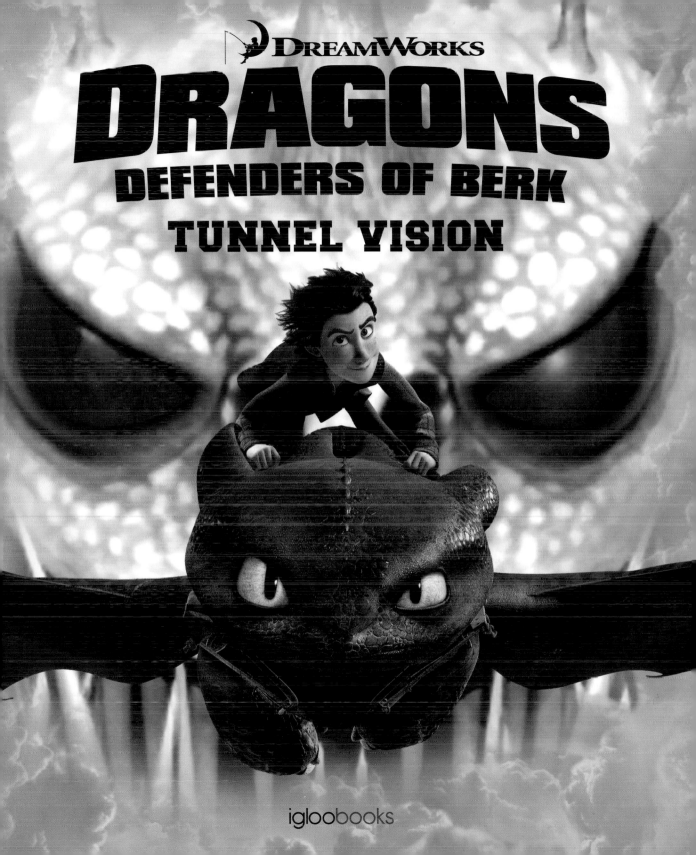

A strange smell wafted through the village of Berk.
It was Gobber's least favourite time of the year... bathtime!
"A Viking is supposed to smell this way!" he cried.
"It's for your own good, Gobber," replied Stoick.
"Actually, Dad, it's for the good of the town!" said Hiccup.
Fishlegs ran to the village well, dropped down a
bucket and started to lift it back out.

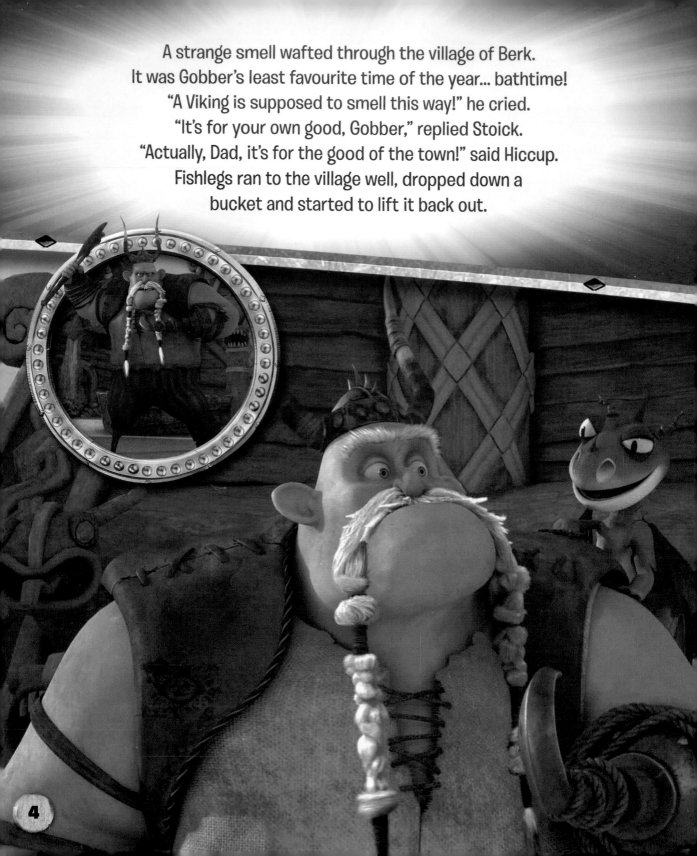

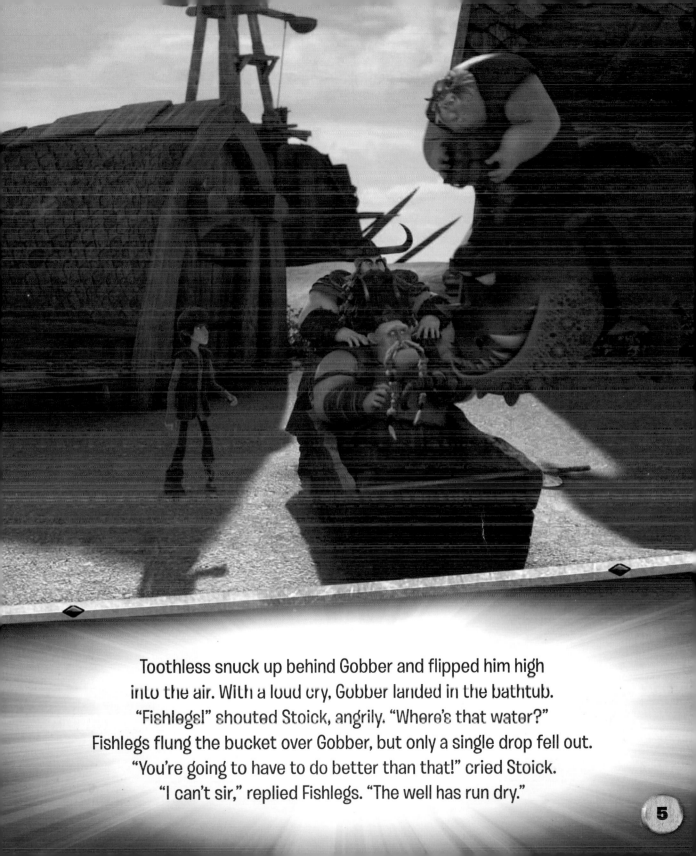

Toothless snuck up behind Gobber and flipped him high
into the air. With a loud cry, Gobber landed in the bathtub.
"Fishlegs!" shouted Stoick, angrily. "Where's that water?"
Fishlegs flung the bucket over Gobber, but only a single drop fell out.
"You're going to have to do better than that!" cried Stoick.
"I can't sir," replied Fishlegs. "The well has run dry."

Stoick looked worried. "We'll have to dig a new well, but until it's done we'll have to ration water," he said. "Astrid, Snotlout, Ruffnut and Tuffnut, go to the mountain streams to collect water," said Hiccup. "Fishlegs, Meatlug, you're going to help me figure out what happened inside that well."

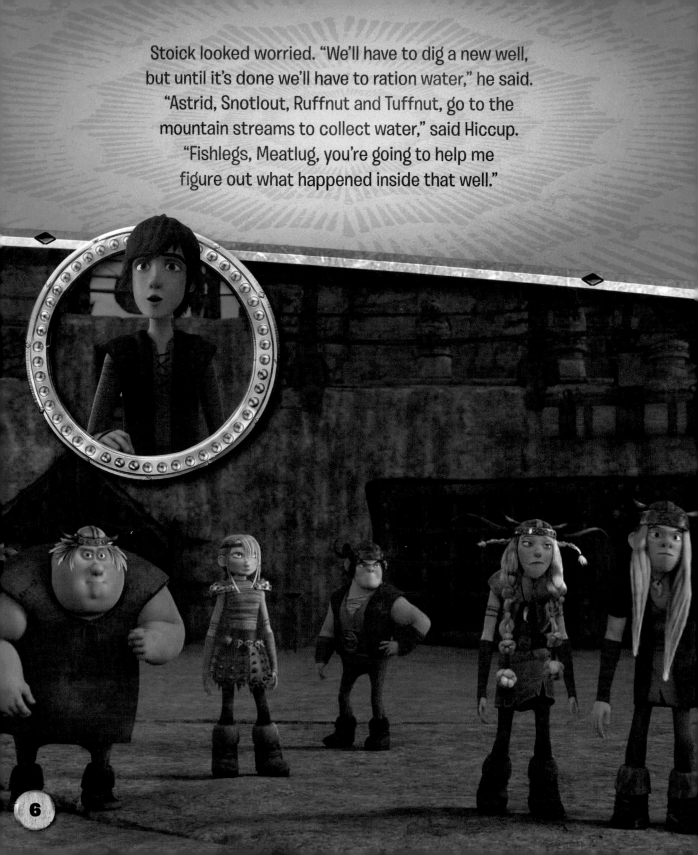

With a rope tied to Meatlug, Hiccup began to make his way
down into the dark, dank well. Just as he was nearing the bottom,
the rope caught on a jagged rock and SNAP! Hiccup fell to the ground.
Toothless flew down after him and just managed to squeeze through.
"We're okay," Hiccup called out, as he dusted himself down.

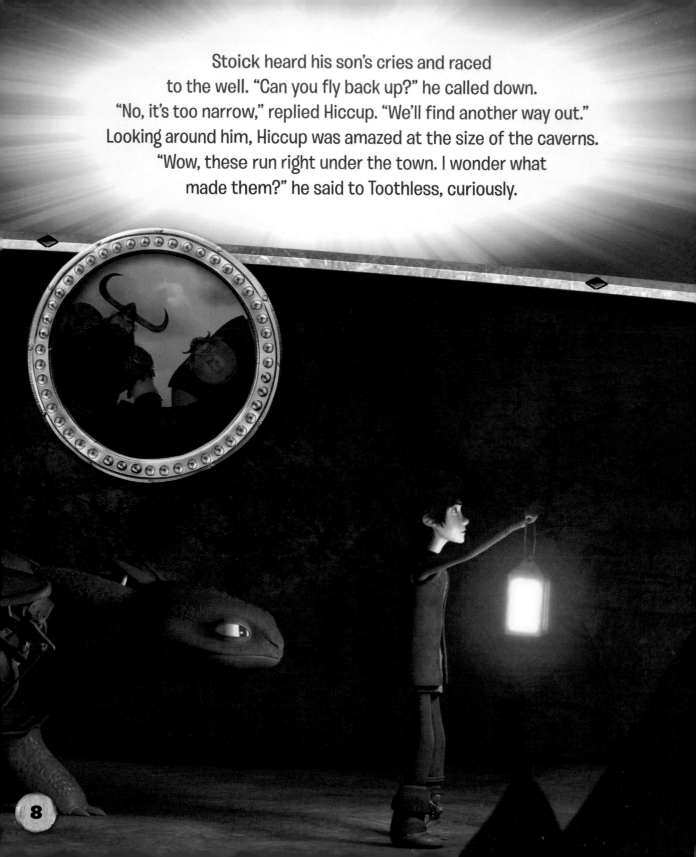

Stoick heard his son's cries and raced
to the well. "Can you fly back up?" he called down.
"No, it's too narrow," replied Hiccup. "We'll find another way out."
Looking around him, Hiccup was amazed at the size of the caverns.
"Wow, these run right under the town. I wonder what
made them?" he said to Toothless, curiously.

As they moved further into the caves, they discovered
a clue - hatched dragon eggs! Suddenly, huge teeth stared them
in the face. Three Whispering Death dragons appeared, but instead of
chasing after Hiccup and Toothless, they began to burrow upwards.
"They're heading to the village! We have to stop them!" cried Hiccup.

Meanwhile, back in the village, Astrid, Snotlout,
Ruffnut and Tuffnut were handing out jugs of water to everyone.
All of a sudden, a Whispering Death ripped through the
rocky ground, baring its sharp fangs at the villagers.
"Stand back!" screamed Gobber, protecting a boy
from the Whispering Death's fiery blast.

The Whispering Deaths fiercely attacked the village, burrowing underground then erupting into the air. "Quickly, everyone! Form a defensive line in the middle of town!" ordered Stoick. As the Vikings prepared to defend their village, Hiccup and Toothless arrived back just in time to join the devastating battle.

As the Vikings defended their village, Hiccup remembered what he had read in the *Book of Dragons*. "Let's shine a little light on the situation," he said, using his shield to reflect the sun's rays into the eyes of the nearest Whispering Death. "It's working, we're driving them away from the village!" cried Astrid. "I don't think this is over yet. Not by a long shot," said Hiccup.

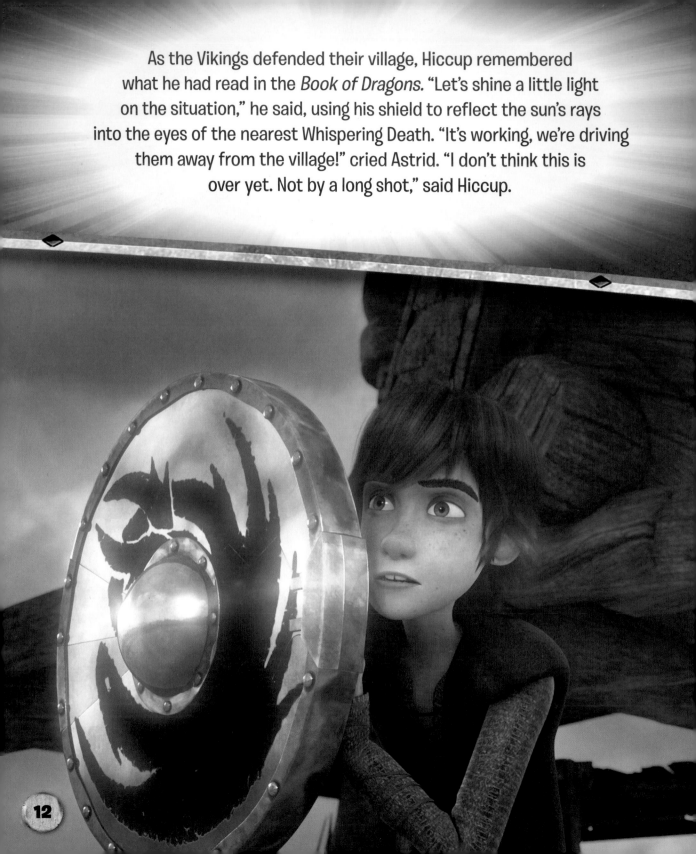

Just then, the ground began to shake and a huge beast,
twice the size of a Whispering Death, exploded into the sky.
"This is exactly what I was afraid of!" cried Hiccup. The enormous
dragon thrashed its tail wildly, sending rocks flying.
"What is that thing?" cried Snotlout.

Hiccup quizzed Fishlegs over the strange dragon.
"Hiccup, I'm certain I would have remembered an all-white,
Boulder-Class, Titan-Wing Whispering Death with bright red eyes
that can bore a hole right through your very soul!" shouted Fishlegs.
Just as the enormous beast got closer, Toothless fired a plasma
blast and the beast let out an ear-splitting scream.

"It's a SCREAMING Death!" shouted Tuffnut, joining his friends
for a closer look. Suddenly, all three Whispering Deaths reappeared.
"Hiccup, what are we going to do?" cried Astrid, panicking.
"You guys focus on the Whispering Deaths. I'll try to keep the
Screaming Death busy," said Hiccup, zooming off.

Toothless fired another plasma blast at the
Screaming Death. BAM! It fought back, flicking its tail and
knocking Hiccup to the ground. Unarmed and without
Toothless to save him, Hiccup was in real trouble.
The beast let out another ear-splitting scream.

Stoick swooped in on Thornado, who shot a sonic
blast straight at the Screaming Death. It screamed, spun and
flew away, giving Hiccup enough time to climb back onto Toothless.
"I don't even want to know what that thing is, but we have to get
it away from here before it does real damage!" yelled Stoick.
"I'll lead it out of the village," Hiccup called back.

"Okay, let's see how it likes this," said Hiccup, using his shield to shine sunlight into the Screaming Death's eyes. The beast hissed and dived underground. Seconds later, it catapulted back out and charged straight at Hiccup and Stoick. "It might not have that weakness like the Whispering Deaths," said Hiccup, feeling confused. "Well, we better figure out what weakness it does have - and quick!" shouted Stoick.

With the Screaming Death getting closer and closer, Hiccup suddenly
realised something. "It's actually attracted to the light," he thought.
"I guess that's a weakness, too. Toothless, head towards the sea stacks!"
The Screaming Death chased Hiccup and Toothless, as they
used the glistening shield to draw it towards the
giant boulders in the sea.

Back in Berk, the Dragon Riders had finally
managed to fight off the Whispering Deaths. Astrid looked up
and saw Hiccup being chased by the huge, beastly Screaming Death.
"Stormfly, quick!" she said, flying up to meet with Hiccup.
"It doesn't have the Whispering Death's weakness. It goes after the
sunlight," shouted Hiccup, as the Screaming Death got closer.

"How do we beat it?" asked Astrid, hoping Hiccup had a plan.
"We give it what it wants! I'll keep it following me. You guys
get behind me and hit it with everything you have," said Hiccup.
Hiccup held his shield up high towards the sun to keep
the Screaming Death hot on his heels.

Hiccup and Toothless zigzagged dangerously between
the towering sea stacks, as the Screaming Death followed them.
Hiccup led it to a huge rock face, swerving clear at the last second.
Smash! It was too late for the Screaming Death and the angry
beast crashed into the rocks, falling down onto a ledge below.
"Its wings are hurt. It can't fly!" cried Hiccup, as the Whispering
Deaths swooped in and carried the Screaming Death away.

The battle was over at last, so the tired
and thirsty Dragon Riders returned to the village.
"You guys, look!" cried Fishlegs. "The well is filling back up."
"The Screaming Death's digging must have created a new channel
for the water to flow back to our well," explained Hiccup.

Standing nearby, Gobber saw the well was full with water again. "Right. Well, I'll be going home now," he said, trying to slip away quietly. "Not so fast, Gobber," said Stoick, grabbing his arm and throwing him into the tub. Fishlegs started to pull on a rope, raising a bucket full of cool, clean water. "Fishlegs, soap and water!" shouted Stoick, as a miserable-looking Gobber had the most unenjoyable bath of his life!